OUR BIG BLUE SOFA

THINGS FOUND
(LAST YEAR)
UNDER THE CUSHIONS OF OUR BIG BLUE SOFA

A pizza crust

The letter G
from the
word game
Scrabble

The instructions
for the
video player

Mum's car keys

A newsletter
from school

A mountain of
biscuit crumbs

Granny Clayton's
bus pass

A dead fly

A moth's wing

The Joker from a
pack of cards

A golf ball

Dad's reading
glasses

Dad's case for
his reading
glasses

A phone bill

Pine needles
from last year's
Christmas tree

2 pieces of
red Lego

A shopping list

A tie –
probably Dad's

A dirty teaspoon

A postcard from
Granny Clayton

Two biros

A pink paperclip

A knitting needle

Binky's
cat collar

A blue button

£100
of Monopoly
money

A pea

If found, please return this book to the sofa.

For Wanda, Ava and Bill
with love

In memory of Irene

I would like to thank
Celia Catchpole and
Emma Harris for
their support and
encouragement.

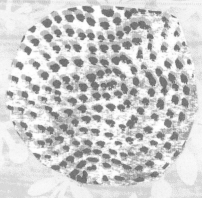

Fossilised Crisp
[Actual Size]

First published 2006 by Macmillan Children's Books
This edition published 2015 by Macmillan Children's Books
an imprint of Pan Macmillan,
20 New Wharf Road, London N1 9RR
Associated companies throughout the world
www.panmacmillan.com

ISBN: 978-1-4472-7676-0

1 3 5 7 9 8 6 4 2

A CIP catalogue record for this book is available from the British Library.

Printed in China

OUR BIG BLUE SOFA

tim hopgood

MACMILLAN CHILDREN'S BOOKS

Our sofa is big and blue.
It's been in our family for
years. No one knows
exactly how old it is, but
I reckon it's older than
my Dad and he's older
than anyone else I know –
apart from Granny Clayton,
and she's nearly a 100!

This is me.
My name is Jessica,
but everyone calls
me Jessy.

And this is my
brother Tom.

One of our favourite things is bouncing on our

big blue sofa.

"Stop that at once!" says Mom.

"Sofas are for sitting on and NOT for bouncing!"

"We're practising for the Sofa Bouncing World Championships!" we explain.

Dad says,
"That sofa's **had it!**
It's **lumpier**
than ever!"

But our two cats
Inky and Binky
don't seem to mind.
And neither do we.
We have great
adventures on our

**big blue
sofa.**

Today Tom and I are
underwater explorers on a
big blue
submarine.

"Has ANYONE
seen the remote
control for the TV?"
asks Dad.

"It's at the bottom of
the ocean," I reply.
"But watch out for
the sharks!"

Emergency!
Here comes the

**big blue
hospital
bed.**

NEE- NAR!

NEE- NAR!

X-RAY DEPT.

EXIT

EYE DEPT.

EMERGENCY DEPT.

I'm busy treating patients for broken bones and infectious diseases.

Granny Clayton says that the big blue sofa is terrible for her bad back. She says she knows a place where Mum and Dad can buy a not-quite-perfect sofa for less than half-price.
But why would we want a not-quite-perfect sofa when we already have a big blue sofa that is absolutely perfect?

Today it's a
big blue hot air balloon
and we're flying high above the clouds.

Dad asks,

"Why are the cushions all over the floor?"

"They're not cushions, they're sandbags," says Tom.

Mum says,

"Well please tidy up the sandbags before tea."

Mum is calling from
the other room,

"TOM! JESSY!
Tea's ready."

We can only just
hear her because
now we're in a

big blue
taxicab

and we're stuck in traffic
on a noisy city street.

After tea, Dad says,

"Come along **you two.** It's time for bed!"

But we're riding through the jungle on the back of a **big blue elephant.**

"Can we stay up?"
asks Tom.
"Elephants don't like
to be rushed."

"Ten more minutes
and then
straight
to bed,"
says Dad.

Disaster!

This morning something awful happened!

While Tom was trying to beat his own World Record for non-stop bouncing, there was a huge thud and the whole room shook.

Our **big blue sofa** isn't bouncy any more.

"Is our sofa going to
be mended?" I ask Mum.
She says that she's
ordered a new one.
But I don't want a
new one.

"I want our big
blue sofa," I say.
"So do I!" says Tom.

Our big blue sofa is missing!

There's just a **big dusty space** where it should be.

Wow!

Look at our **brand new sofa!**

"Don't forget,
NO bouncing
on the **brand
new sofa,"**

says Mum.

It's huge!
It's so big that
it makes the
cats look like
kittens again.

Our **brand new sofa** is so big, there's enough room on it for all our friends. Granny Clayton says we've probably broken a World Record for the-most-friends-on-a-sofa-at-any-one-time.

And best of all . . .

. . . every now and then,
when no one's looking,
it makes a fantastic
trampoline.

We're busy practising for the

Sofa Olympics!

"TOM! JESSY! Stop bouncing!"

THINGS
FOUND
(RECENTLY)
UNDER THE
CUSHIONS OF
OUR BRAND
NEW SOFA

12 pieces of
popcorn

A pink sock

The letter Z
from the
word game
SCRABBLE

The instructions
for the DVD
player

Mum's car keys

Dad's reading
glasses

Dad's case for his
reading
glasses

Found anything interesting under your sofa's cushions?

Now
that's got
to be a
WORLD
RECORD!

tjmhopgood